AROUND FRED'S BED

by Manus Pinkwater

pictures by Robert Mertens

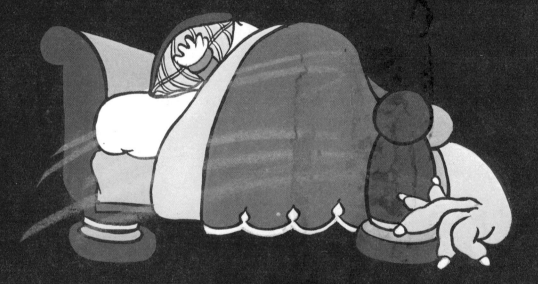

Prentice-Hall, Inc., Englewood Cliffs, New Jersey

Text Copyright © 1976 by Manus Pinkwater
Illustrations copyright © 1976 by Robert Mertens

Printed in the United States of America

Prentice-Hall International, Inc., London
Prentice-Hall of Australia, Pty. Ltd., North Sydney
Prentice-Hall of Canada, Ltd., Toronto
Prentice-Hall of India Private Ltd., New Delhi
Prentice-Hall of Japan, Inc., Tokyo

10   9   8   7   6   5   4   3   2   1

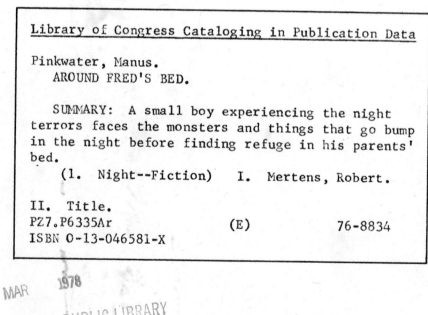

Library of Congress Cataloging in Publication Data

Pinkwater, Manus.
    AROUND FRED'S BED.

    SUMMARY: A small boy experiencing the night
terrors faces the monsters and things that go bump
in the night before finding refuge in his parents'
bed.
    (1. Night--Fiction)   I. Mertens, Robert.

II. Title.
PZ7.P6335Ar   (E)   76-8834
ISBN 0-13-046581-X

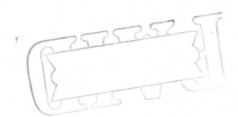

for Rohanna,
    Steven,
        and Dahlia

This is Fred's room.

This is Fred's bed.

This is Fred.

Fred was having a bad dream.

Fred woke up.

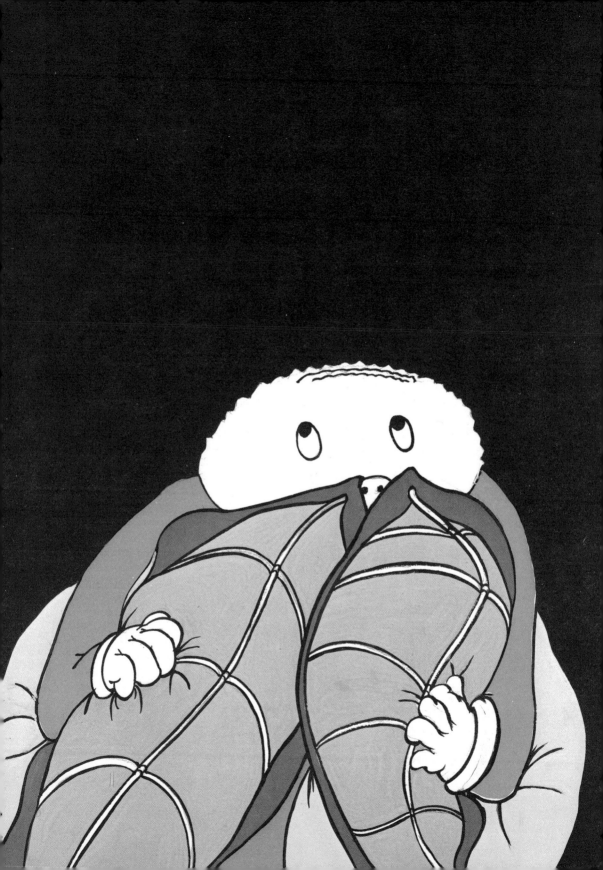

The things from his dream were
still there.

"Get out. Get out. Get out of here. Get out," Fred said.

The things just grinned and did not move.

"If you don't go, I will," Fred told them.

There were things in the hall, too.

"I'm going to tell my mommy."

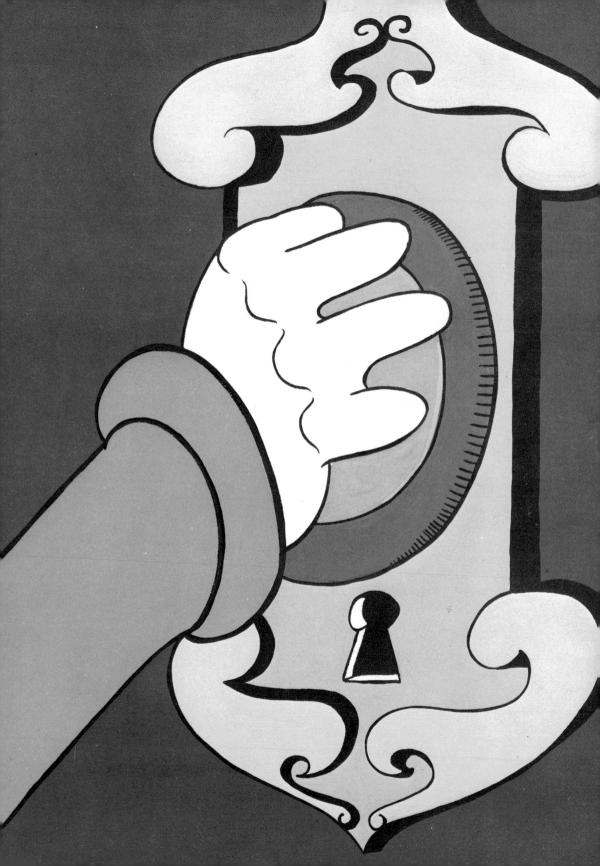

"Mommy, Daddy, wake up. There are monsters in my room."

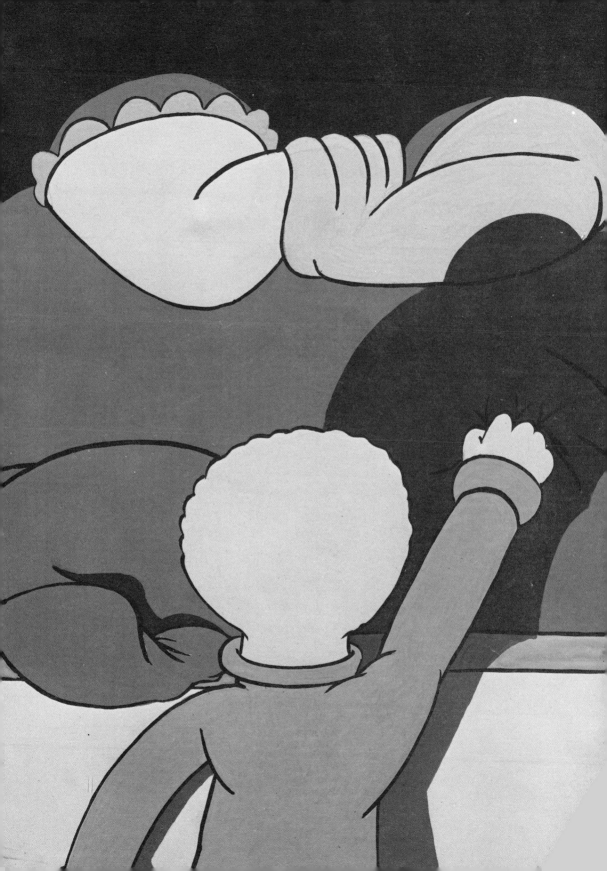

"There are no monsters here,"
said Daddy.

"Get into bed with us."

Good night.